HAPPY ISLAND
AND THE
TYPHOONS

HAPPY ISLAND AND THE TYPHOONS

Antonia Babauta Lyzenga

ARPress
ILLUMINATING IDEAS
EMPOWERING VOICES

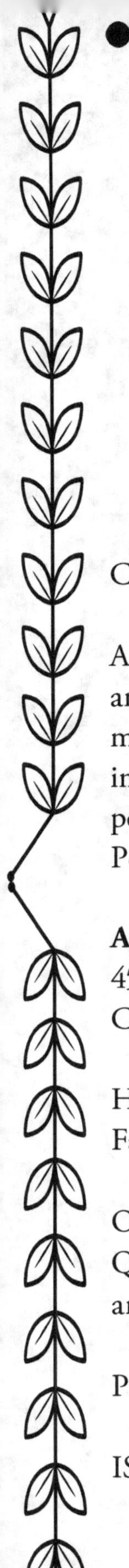

ARPress
45 Dan Road Suite 5
Canton MA 02021

Hotline: 1(888) 821-0229
Fax: 1(508) 545-7580

Ordering Information:
Quantity sales. Special discounts are available on quantity purchases by corporations, associations, and others. For details, contact the publisher at the address above.

Printed in the United States of America.

ISBN-13:   Softcover   979-8-89676-500-4
                eBook   979-8-89676-501-1

Library of Congress Control Number: 2022900332

Dedication

I dedicate this book to my children Katrina DeJong Shockley, Gerrit Glen Lyzenga and Kelly Harmen Lyzenga, who have given me so much joy and purpose in life.

You Are My Sister

You are my sister the only one to me.
You are leaving the nest a baby bird set free.
You are my sister it seems like yesterday
You are going to the yard with your dolls to play.
You are my sister the times have quickly passed,
You have your memories special ones that last.
You are my sister a sister that is true.
You are always in my heart, remember I love you.
You are my sister the world you need to see,
Go into the world baby bird spread your wings, be free.

Kelly Lyzenga

Happy Island and the Typhoons

Deno and his ten year old sister Lela knelt on the damp ground and stared at the rubble where their home once stood. They were stunned at the sight before their eyes. Their home had disappeared. Earlier, the children were also informed that their parents were likely lost at sea.

Homeless and heart broken, Lela sobbed and as tears ran down her cheeks she cried, "O-o-oh Deno, what are we going to do? Our house is gone and we might never see Mother and Father again. I'm scared." Deno put his left hand on Lela's shoulder, squeezed it lightly and said, "We'll be just fine. I'll take care of you."

He made a fist with his right hand and ran it up and down his right leg as he muttered, " Mother and Father must have been overwhelmed by the giant waves and strong wind that overturned the proa."

Two days earlier a great typhoon came and swept away homes, trees, and whatever was in its way. The loss of their parents and the devastation before their eyes was so great that the children felt utterly helpless. They seemed to be frozen on the spot for a time.

When the typhoon warning sounded the children knew where to seek for shelter from past typhoons. They bundled their clothes and ran up the hill where they were always welcomed by their neighbors, Mr. and Mrs. Cruse. During the storm Lela and Deno were fortunate to be safe in their neighbor's home. The house was nestled on the hillside partially sheltered from the storm.

They huddled in the living room with their friends, surrounded by heavy furniture. Whenever they heard a coconut tree snap and break, or saw objects flying in the air, they rushed to get under tables and chairs for safety. The howling wind and streams of water running down from the roof of the house continued for days, with only short breaks. Both children and adults took catnaps which was the usual practice. Everyone was warned to be ready to find a safe place in case the wind changed its course and hit the vulnerable side of the house.

To pass the time the children played quietly with strings, making shapes with their fingers and playing with other homemade toys. These were tense and fearful moments, so the adults whispered words of comfort. Each day went by and the group waited to see what was going to happen. A sense of relief came only whenever someone laughed or giggled.

The wind subsided and the rain ceased. Mr. Cruse opened a window and the children rushed over to join him to view what the typhoon had damaged. They could only see debris against the window. Mr. Cruse told his two children along with Deno and Lela to move the furniture back to their usual places before they could go outside. As they were finishing up they heard a knock on the door. Mr. Cruse opened it and two men started to speak to him. Deno, Lela and the other children squeezed by the men and walked outside.

"Oh no! " cried Lela. " Wow wee! "Exclaimed her girlfriend.

Deno and his friend shook their heads in disbelief and walked around looking at the pile of wood and other broken articles. Eagerly Deno and Lela decided to run home and see what happened to their house. They packed their bags and thanked Mr. and Mrs. Cruse for keeping them safe, but before Deno completed his sentence, Mr. Cruse announced to the children that the men who spoke to him had been searching for survivors since early that morning. They did not find anyone.

"If there was anybody fishing and was caught during the storm he or she may have been swept out to sea," said one of the men.

Deno turned to Lela and said, "Surely, Mother and Father saw the storm coming. They were supposed to be fishing beyond the reef for big fish, but they should still have had time to return to shore," trying to reassure Lela. Lela put her hands on her mouth and became very quiet.

The children, not fully understanding what happened to their parents hurried down the hill toward their home. In their confusion, and feeling abandoned they walked until they reached the spot where their house used to be. There, they dropped on their knees and began to sob.

Later when they realized what may have happened to their parents, they sat down on the damp ground and began to think about their future.

"Maybe Aunt Mina and Uncle Hector have heard about what happened here," Deno said chocking up and looking at Lela

"Yes, I think they should have," Lela answered, wiping her face with the upper part of her sleeve.

"I hope they come for us soon. Right now we have to go back to Mr. and Mrs. Cruse and tell them about our house," stated Deno.

Reluctantly, the children stood up and started to walk. Glancing back every now and then the children walked away. They left the place where their once cherished home was before the typhoon

"Our house is blown away and only part of the floor is there," said Deno, as he spoke to Mr. Cruse. Mr. Cruse looked at the children and said, "Both of you can have a home here with my family. You should know that by now."

Deno and Lela were so glad and grateful to have such caring family friends. Deno and Lela stayed with Mr. Cruse and his family for a week. Friends and neighbors searched daily for Deno and Lela's parents but they were never found.

In the meantime Aunt Mina and Uncle Hector received news concerning the natural disaster on Happy Island. They inquired about their relatives. Sadly they heard that Deno and Lela had lost their parents and were living with family friends, Mr. and Mrs. Cruse. Uncle Hector and Aunt Mina left their two children with a neighbor and immediately took off in their proa, their native canoe, to find Deno and Lela. They took extra food and other necessities for Mr. Cruse and his family. Aunt Mina remembered how difficult it was to receive certain foods and medical supplies from the surrounding islands when big typhoons occurred. When they arrived on Happy Island, Aunt Mina and Uncle Hector were so glad to see the children and were amazed to observe how much they had grown, both in stature and character. They persevered and managed to survive the possible death of their parents and the loss of their home. Accepting responsibilities and helping each other clearly prepared Deno and Lela to meet this crisis in their lives.

The children bid their friends goodbye and thanked Mr. and Mrs. Cruse for their kindness. They left with their aunt and uncle looking forward to a new life. As the family was sailing to Cherika Island, Aunt Mina spoke to Deno about his and Lela's future. She also explained to him that he and Lela could stay with her as long as they wished. The family traveled the whole day. When they reached their new island home Deno and Lela were utterly surprised to see such a large village. There was so much to discover on Chirika Island where Aunt Mina and her family lived.

"I can find work and earn some money to help with your cleft palate operation that Aunt Mina said you can have, on our way over here," Deno whispered to Lela.

"And I can do housework or do something to help the family too," said Lela, eagerly as she smiled then covered her mouth.

Apparently, now, the children were ready to face a new life in a new home.

Kin and Anna, the children's parents, were caught at the middle of a raging ocean. When they saw the dark, angry clouds heading closer and closer to Happy Island, with whipping winds and heavy rain coming down, they turned to the opposite direction where they could see the deeper and calmer waters. Kin faced the proa away from Happy Island towards the unknown to find safety. Anna tied down all their fishing equipment and put away their tools, including extra roll of fishing net material, two small knives, a machete, bamboo containers of water, gourds for bailing, four tortillas and fried fish for lunch.

Suddenly the drenching rain increased and the mighty, gusty wind blew on the proa's sail. The proa went flying over the waves carried by the great wind and the strong current. Kin and Anna lay facing down, holding tightly to the sides of the canoe, and gripping on to each other's hand. As the canoe sped on with the current, Kin and Anna lifted their heads every now and then to see where they were heading. In the confusion, they lost their sense of direction. They only saw more rain and wave after wave of ocean water. The wind and ocean current were in control and Kin and Anna lay helpless in their proa. They looked at each other and knew what needed to be done with the water accumulating quickly. As they unclasped their hands, they reached for their gourd scoops and began to bail the water out of the canoe.

Many more hours went by and the storm became calm, but the ocean current continued to carry them on its natural course. Slowly the clouds parted and the couple saw a ray of light from the sun. Instinctively Kin knew in what direction they were heading. Since this is typhoon season they were carried by the ocean current

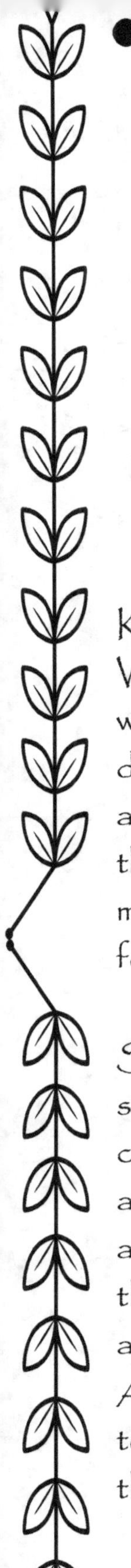

due east where most of the foreign ships had journeyed before to reach the other side of the world.

Soon the sun began to set and darkness surrounded them, but the stars began to shine as the clouds parted. Kin and Anna now felt relief for they could estimate about where they were in the massive ocean. They knew how to read the sky from the lessons their parents taught them when they were little. The wind and the current continued to push them on in their proa, now with a torn sail.

Suddenly they saw a huge form before their eyes and realized that they were approaching land. Kin picked up his oar and rowed tirelessly until they reached a sandy shore.

"I think we will be safer if we spend the rest of the night here in our proa," stated Kin. Anna replied, "I agree with you. Do you notice that it is strangely quiet? I can only hear night creatures making noises."

"I know, we'll see where we are in the morning," said Kin.

The exhausted couple settled for the night. As they closed their eyes they thought of the places they would discover on this island.

The bright, warm sunlight touched their faces and slowly they opened their eyes the next morning. As they looked around everything seemed calm and quiet. Only the sound of the ocean waves attracted their attention. With anticipation, they jumped out of their proa and walked hurriedly to find something for breakfast. The tortillas and fish they brought were spoiled and Anna had to throw them away. Kin found a coconut tree, climbed it and cut down two green coconuts for their meal. Afterward they safely put the proa under a tree and covered it with leafy branches. Taking the necessary supplies with them, they walked off to look over the island. As they moved along they noticed how similar the new place was to their home on Happy Island. The volcanic rocks, plants, insects and animals were just like where Kin and Anna lived. Soon they found a small stream flowing down from the side of a lush

green knoll. They stopped, drank the clear, cool fresh water and swam in the deeper part of the stream. They rested for a while and then continued walking, observing the tropical plants, and the colorful birds of orange, red and yellow plumage, as they searched for any sign of human life. They traveled for most of the day looking for inhabitants until they reached the other side of the island. Unfortunately, they found no other people. They became resigned to the idea that they were the only ones safely swept to that island by the great typhoon.

Kin and Anna decided to search for some food for dinner. Anna picked some bananas and dug up two taro roots. Kin caught two small fish and cleaned them. Then he took his machete, struck a lava rock several times, creating sparks then he built a fire. They cooked their food, ate and rested. As the sun began to set they looked for a safe place to spend the night. They decided to go back to the cave they saw earlier as they were walking. When they arrived at the cave they made a bed from coconut leaves. Before they closed their eyes Anna was overcome with loneliness for their children and wept.

"I really miss Lela and Deno. I hope that they are with our friends, as we told them to do during other typhoons," said Anna

Kin turned on his side, close to Anna and whispered, "I know they are fine. Deno knows what to do when he hears a typhoon warning." Anna felt better and both fell asleep.

The sound of rain woke them up in the morning. They quickly grabbed their bamboo water containers and placed each of them under large, breadfruit leaves to catch some fresh water. The rain finally stopped and Kin went out and returned with ripe bananas and some green coconuts.

As they relished the soft, sweet coconut meat, Kin said, "When we are finished with breakfast, let's start repairing the proa . Then when it's done we will sail home."

Anna happily agreed. "Yes! Oh, Yes! We have to get back home. The children and our friends are most likely worried about us," said Anna.

So, Kin and Anna worked daily on the proa. Patiently Kin and Anna chopped down pagu trees, ripped off the stringy bark from top to bottom, dried them and intra-wove the fibers with the fishing net to repair the sail. The tedious work took so much time. Months went by before the sail was completed. Next, the broken proa balance needed to be replaced. Kin searched for the right tree. Finally he found one and began to shape it. During his leisure time when Kin saw the tall, straight and strong trees, he thought about building a simple airy hut at the beach. He cut down the extra logs he would need for the hut so that he and Anna could sleep at night there instead of in the musty cave.

They did not think about the time only about returning home to Happy Island and reuniting with their children. Kin and Anna labored daily repairing the proa, and now they were living in their cool, breezy hut on the beach. Each day when they were not working on the proa they took time to discover a new part of the island. One day they saw an area just perfect for swimming and diving. Kin did not wait long to try his diving skills. Anna waited at the shallow part. Soon Kin came up to Anna with a handful of oyster shells. He left Anna's side and came back with his knife. He pried open one oyster shell and to their surprise there was a beautiful, rare, black pearl before their eyes! Kin pried open the other oyster shells and found big, black pearls in each of them!

Kin looked deeply into Anna's eyes and said, "I think I'll build you the biggest and the most beautiful house on Happy Island when we get home."

Anna, with tears in her eyes said, "My only wish is that our Lela would get the best care when the doctors operate on her face. A set of beautiful, straight teeth and a little scar on her lip would be all she would want."

Kin answered eagerly, "That too. We'll take care of our children and use our money from the sale of the pearls wisely. I plan to dive for more pearls each day until we are ready to leave this island."

With big dreams and happy hearts Kin and Anna went home to their simple hut, worked on the proa balance, and Kin dived for pearls.

Weeks and months went by and then it became a year. The couple harvested more black pearls and finished the repairs on the proa. Kin and Anna were ready to sail home. At the last moment Kin remembered that they needed extra ropes to tie down their supplies and emergency lines for the sail. He left the next morning to cut some pagu trees to make the ropes. By noon Anna was worried when Kin did not return. She left her chores and went searching for Kin. As she walked she called out for him.

She finally heard him calling her name. She rushed to his side where he was resting against a coconut tree. He was hurt!

"I was cutting the pagu tree when the machete slipped out of my hand and cut me right here below the knee," Kin pointed at his leg.

Anna could see blood on Kin's leg where he wrapped it with soft leaves and tied it with some vines. She assisted him up as she said, "Let's go home. I will take good care of your leg."

Kin limped slowly home, leaning on Anna as she led the way. When they reached their hut on the beach, Anna cleaned and applied her pasty, crushed, herb leaves on Kin's cut and bandaged it.

She watched Kin as he struggled to heal, sleeping each day and night. Eventually some infection set in and the fever left him helpless. Anna remained calm, which was her nature and nursed Kin. She was frugal with food and water since she didn't want to leave Kin's bedside. Several weeks went by and Kin was able to hop around on his right foot. He wanted so much to sail home to Happy Island, but his injury prevented him and Anna from leaving. Besides that, they enjoyed the warm weather and tranquil life. Gradually, months came and went and another year passed.

While Kin was recovering from his injury, another great typhoon came and destroyed the sail on the proa and their hut. Sadly they returned to live in the old musty cave.

With determination, Kin returned to the jungle and chopped some more wood to rebuild their hut and pagu trees for fibers to make a new sail for the proa. The time consuming tasks of repairing the proa and finding food kept Kin and Anna busy. Kin was also determined on diving for more black pearls. He dived and harvested as many pearls as he could. Then he finished repairing the proa. Finally they completed all their tasks

As Kin and Anna were walking to the beach the next day, Anna turned to Kin and said, "I feel like I am going to die on this island without seeing our children again. We have to get back to Happy Island."

Kin stood still, took Anna's hands and placed them on his cheeks and replied," You are right. We must go home. I miss our children too."

Hurriedly they gathered food, filled their bamboo water containers with fresh water, placed their tools in the canoe and waited for the right time to sail to Happy Island. As they waited, they put the black pearls in small, fiber bags and tied them along the inside of the proa. They also planned to wear a belt and tie a bag of pearls on each side of their hips. If the proa should capsize and they had to swim, Kin and Anna would still have some of their black pearls. Anxiously they waited for the strong ocean current heading westward to take them back home.

After working day after day mending fishing nets for other fishermen and saving his money for three years, Deno stood in Aunt Mina's living room with Lela and said, "I spoke to a doctor and made an appointment for you to see him about the surgery on your mouth. It is tomorrow! Then on your next visit he would perform the surgery and make you look so beautiful!"

Lela, now a shy teen looked at Deno, wide eyed and said, "You know, you are the best brother in the world!" and burst out laughing and hugging Deno.

"I only want you to feel good about yourself and be happy," he said, pulling her hands down to her sides.

Lela could hardly contain herself, so she rushed off to find Aunt Mina and tell her the great news. Aunt Mina, Uncle Hector and her cousins were so pleased that Lela was having her cleft palate surgery. They had seen how unhappy Lela was staying home year after year refusing to be seen in public because of her cleft palate. The jeers and rejections of her peers were too painful to bear. She hid herself from the public by staying home. She learned to read with Aunt Mina who tutored her after Lela's chores were done. Lela was happy with her books.

The next week Deno took Lela to the hospital to see Dr. Toon, the surgeon who was to perform the surgery. While she was waiting for her doctor a young boy her age with a clubfoot started talking to her.

"My adopted father was a governor on Happy Island years ago," Rafe told Lela.

"My brother and I used to live on Happy Island but we are orphans now, and we live with our Aunt Mina here," stated Lela. Rafe, who seemed fond of Lela turned pale and moved away from her.

"My adopted father said that I am not supposed to speak to anyone who is from Happy Island. They are cruel and evil people," Rafe blurted out. After a long pause Rafe told Lela why his adopted father left Happy Island and how he found a new home. Then he turned and went with a nurse who just called his name to see his doctor. Lela also went with a nurse into an office where the nurse took personal information about her, and then the nurse took some blood from her arm. There were other tests done and then Lela and Deno went home.

Another week went by and it was time for Lela's surgery. Deno and Lela went to the hospital where they were to meet Dr. Toon. As they were passing by the waiting room Lela saw Rafe again. He waved at her. She remembered him, the boy with the clubfoot.

As Lela made her visits to the hospital to see Dr. Toon, she saw Rafe waved and watched her as she walked away. At her next visit she did not see him. She looked for him at each visit to the hospital after her successful surgery, but no Rafe. He seemed to just disappear. She thought of him often and wondered what happened to the only boy who was kind to her. Now that her surgery was a success and her face was healing she dreamed of having a family of her own. Lela remembered her parents and thought how good it was to have a loving and caring home.

Rafe's foot surgery was a complete success. He was fitted with a special pair of shoes then his adopted father sent him north to the largest hospital on Chirika Island. While he was there Rafe was under the care of a doctor who trained Rafe in an area of medical science. He was a bright and ambitious student who was always busy. Suddenly he realized that he finally completed his first year of training. During internship he chose to become a pharmacist. He was lonely and eager to complete his studies and return home. So, with determination and focus on his work Rafe accomplished his goal and was ready to become a professional pharmacist.

In the meantime Lela became a volunteer at the hospital where she and Rafe each had their surgeries. Later she was hired as Dr. Toon's aide. The doctor was extremely impressed with Lela's medical knowledge. He later learned that while Lela was home bound she studied many medical manuals provided by the nurses who were sent to care for the poor in the villages.

Still hoping to see Rafe one day if he should visit the hospital, Lela anxiously looked forward to being at work. Even after many young, island boys begged to take her out to lunch, she refused. Her heart belonged to Rafe, the boy she remembered telling her about his clubfoot and spending time together.

Rafe returned home and applied for the hospital Pharmacy and was accepted. He was back at the hospital where he had his foot surgery and remembered the kind nurses. He also remembered Lela, the friendly girl who had cleft palate. She had difficulty speaking, but she was cheerful and spoke kindly about his clubfoot.

"I am wondering, do you remember a young girl by the name Lela?" Rafe asked one of the nurses at the hospital.

The nurse replied, "I am sorry. I am new here and I don't remember a girl named Lela." Rafe continued to inquire, but with no result. Gradually he abandoned his search.

One day he met Mia at a co-worker's birthday party. He was mesmerized by her beauty and he enjoyed Mia's company. He later learned that she came from a very affluent family. They dated for some time and then they became engaged. Lela's name faded in the back of Rafe's mind.

One afternoon Dr. Toon's nurse and Lela went to lunch at the hospital cafeteria. Accidently, Rafe bumped into Lela as they were picking up their food. They both stared at each other and at that moment they recognized a very strong attraction and familiarity.

"Sorry… I bumped you with my elbow. And I… feel like… I know you." Rafe stammered.

Lela, who didn't realized she was holding her breath let it out slowly and touched her mouth, tapping at the tiny scar.

"That is OK, no harm done," replied Lela, as her heart pounded wildly. She knew that she finally found Rafe.

"Who is this enchanting girl with a tiny scar on her mouth?" Rafe said to himself quietly. Before he could say anything else he knew that she had captured his heart. Lela smiled and said," Do you remember a little girl who had a cleft pa…," but before she completed her sentence Rafe put his finger on her lips to stop her.

"Don't say anything more. I have been searching for you since I returned from medical training. I am now a pharmacist in this hospital," Rafe eagerly told her.

"And you were the boy who had the club…," and pointed down at Rafe's feet. Both burst out laughing as they moved toward the table and chairs where Dr. Toon's nurse sat. She stared at the couple and somehow knew that Lela had found a soul mate. All three finished their lunch and Lela promised to meet Rafe again the next day. They enjoyed many afternoons together at the cafeteria and at the beach. Soon Rafe and Lela found themselves falling in love.

One day after lunch Rafe looked at Lela and said, "I am engaged to a girl named Mia." Lela's heart shattered. She covered her face and thought she had lost Rafe.

"Are you going to marry her?" Lela whispered.

"No, you are the one I am going to marry, but Mia will definitely be very angry when I tell her about you. Mia's family is very wealthy and influential and would not appreciate being bested by an orphan. I will convince her to break the engagement right away," Rafe told Lela lovingly.

The next time Rafe and Lela met he told her that Mia was extremely furious and insisted on a wedding date for the two of them to be married. She informed her parents that as soon as the priest agreed to perform the ceremony, she and Rafe would be wed. Rafe felt trapped but continued to see Lela. As for Lela, she cherished every moment she could have with Rafe

Kin and Anna finally arrived on Happy Island one day before dark. They hardly recognized where their house was before. Overgrown weeds and young tree growths covered the house foundation and the yard. They were so deeply overwhelmed by the sight that they reached for each other for comfort. Then with yearning hearts and a glow of hope they looked up beside the hill at Mr. Cruse's house and started to walk up the hill. They wanted to find and hold their children close to their heart.

As Kin and Anna came close to the house, the door quickly opened with Mr. and Mrs. Cruse rushing out to meet them. The women embraced each other and cried.

"We thought you were both dead when you disappeared." cried Mrs. Cruse.

The men shook hands, cleared their throat and Mr. Cruse said, "When we couldn't find your bodies we gave up looking for you. We searched for weeks but then we finally ended it. By the way, your children are fine. They are living with their Aunt Mina and her husband. I heard that they are doing very well." concluded Mr. Cruse.

For hours the four friends exchanged stories relating to the lost years they had experienced. Then before parting to their beds Kin and Anna revealed to their friends the fortune they acquired in black pearls. They discussed how and where to sell the pearls then they went to bed.

Two days later Mr. Cruse took Kin and Anna to the biggest pearl trader on the island where they sold the bags of pearls, except six bags. They reserved four bags for Deno and Lela for their inheritance and two bags for themselves as mementoes of their stay on their little island. Unexpectedly, they became one of the wealthiest families on Happy Island. The villagers were extremely glad to know that they were alive and that they also found their fortune.

Eager to reunite with their children Kin and Anna planned to leave as soon as they made plans to have a house built, before they return from Chirika Island with Lela and Deno. So, gladly the village Commissioner volunteered to oversee the work on the house, in exchange for Kin and Anna's offer to build a larger medical clinic that was needed in the village. As soon as the building plans were finalized Anna and Kin sailed one morning in their proa, hoping to see their children soon. They arrived at Aunt Mina's house in the evening while the family was having their meal. As Anna and Kin entered the dining room, Aunt Mina turned pale with shock and then relief to see her sister still alive. Lela stood up and slowly walked into her mother's arms, with tears in both their eyes. They held on to each other as if they would never let go.

"Oh, how beautiful you are! The doctor definitely gave you a new face," Anna whispered as she caressed Lela's cheeks, choking back her tears.

"Are you happy . . . my Lela?" Anna asked.

"Yes, mother, very happy!" Lela replied between sniffles. Aunt Mina stood up and joined them in their joyous reunion. Kin, Deno, and Uncle Hector shook hands and sat down, asking and answering questions all at once. In the aftermath, everyone was over the shock of the unexpected visit. The family ate a hearty meal and spent the rest of the evening recalling what had occurred in their lives over the past years.

At last Anna looked at Aunt Mina and Uncle Hector and said, "I give you two all the credit and much appreciation for taking care of Lela and Deno during our absence. We thank you for all you've done." Aunt Mina replied, "You should know that we will always care and protect our family.

Next, Kin and Anna faced the family. Kin took a deep breath and said, "Deno, we are a very wealthy family now. We will have the biggest and most beautiful house when we arrive home. You will never have to work so hard again. You are the most caring brother and had to sacrifice so much. Your mother and I love and cherish you for your admirable nature and duty to our family and to your aunt and uncle. We will remain here until our house is ready to occupy. In the meantime your mother and I just want to be close to all of you and be a family again."

During the stay at Aunt Mina and Uncle Hector's home Deno told his parents about Lela and Rafe's relationship. Gradually Kin and Anna became acquainted with Rafe but did not reveal to him anything about their wealth. The family made a pact to keep it a secret. Near the end of their stay on Chirika Island Anna took Lela for a walk on the beach.

As they walked Anna said, "Lela, your father and I came to take you and Deno home to Happy Island. We will have a new home and be a family."

"But I can't leave my friends and my work. I am happy here," Lela replied.

"I understand how you feel dear Lela, but you are not of age to live by yourself. And you cannot live with your Aunt Mina any more. You do not need to work and you can develop many friendships back on Happy Island," Anna said quietly.

By the time they reached the house Lela was terribly unhappy. She wanted to be with her family yet she did not want to leave Rafe behind. Kin called to Lela to sit beside him so they could talk.

"Deno found out that Rafe is engaged to another girl named Mia and he told me and your mother. We would like to see Rafe resolve this problem before you get too deeply involved with him," Kin reasoned with Lela.

"I love him father, and I will do anything to help him," replied Lela.

Kin continued, "Then let us go home and wait until he is free and our family would gladly welcome a fine pharmacist to be your husband. Just remember that according to our custom engagements are difficult to break. Rafe must dearly pay for his commitment to the engagement. A large payment in money and goods must be paid to the betrothed's parents," said Kin, then he left Lela to think about what he just said.

After living on Chirika Island for six months, Kin received a message informing him and the family that their house on Happy Island was ready. Everyone was excited about the news except Lela. She was reluctant to leave Rafe behind. But upon the promise that he may visit the family on Happy Island, Lela agreed to return home.

The pain in Lela's heart at leaving Rafe on Chirika Island somehow lessened when she gazed at the limestone hacienda that was to be her home. Memories of this island also made her feel complete and safe.

The hacienda was furnished with all the essentials and extras to make the family feel comfortable. Next Anna hired three housemaids and a cook. One maid was to be a companion to Lela and do light chores. The other two were to do the more extensive housekeeping.

The rest of the family now had time to bond and enjoy each other's company. Anna and Lela grew closer each day. They had time to go to the village clinic and volunteer teaching young mothers about health care for infants and healthy eating habits. In addition they helped the village nurse distribute medical manuals and health pamphlets to the poor just as the other nurse did when Lela was younger. They also watched as workers built the new clinic which Kin and Anna donated financially.

There were numerous things happening in Lela's life so she decided to keep a journal, and when she wrote to Rafe she included some of her activities. She deeply missed him and as a result letters of endearment sailed in proas back and forth between the two islands.

Rafe, unfortunately had to listen to Mia's insistence about marriage or have him face her parents, renege on his word and pay the engagement penalty. He was furious at the ultimatum and began to save his wages to make the payment.

Early one morning as Rafe was getting ready to go to work he heard something slammed against the side of his house. He looked out his living room window and saw gusts of wind blowing and coconut trees swaying in the wind. Then the heavy rain came pouring down.

"Typhoon!" He shouted as he shut the windows.

"I must secure the medical supplies and be at the pharmacy in case patients need their medicine," he said to himself. Then he raced to the hospital, fighting his way against the dangerous elements. His raincoat and hood protected him from the pouring rain, but the ferocious wind and flying objects forced him to bend down almost touching his knees, fighting his way through the wind. Finally, he reached the hospital and went immediately to the pharmacy securing the supplies. Then he waited for his customers. Some came and returned home quickly. Rafe found comfort behind the counter listening to the roaring wind and rushing rain. He felt safe there at the large hospital, but wondered about Lela and her family. Lately, he thought of her more often than usual. Now he wondered if she was safe from this typhoon.

As the blustering wind blew, Lela stared at the giant waves down at the beach from her front window. It reminded her of the monstrous waves that took her parents from her for several years. Instinctively, she rushed to her parents' bedroom door and knocked.

"Come in, the door is unlocked," her parents called out. They were sitting in bed listening to the roaring wind when Lela stepped inside the opulent bedroom. They motioned for her to sit close to them on the bed.

"I just wanted to see you both before I go downstairs for breakfast," Lela confessed. Anna reached for her and held Lela for a moment. Anna saw the fear and concern in Lela's eyes and guessed that Lela might be thinking about the typhoon that took them away from her.

Half asleep Deno woke up when he heard the strong wind from his opened window. He quickly dressed in his khaki shorts and ran down to the beach. As he observed the giant waves he knew that they were signs of an oncoming typhoon. He looked up at his new home safely by the cliff and felt assured that it would be safe from the storm. Hurriedly the family ate their breakfast then sat by the window and watched as the wind strip coconut trees, uproot vegetation and carry away debris.

The typhoon lasted for only two days, but caused enough damage to the village homes. The limestone hacienda remained unscathed by the storm. The new medical clinic only needed a new roof and new paneling on one side of the building.

Across the ocean on Chirika Island Rafe was so relieved when the winds and the rain came to an end. There was little damage to the hospital building, but small homes and huts were destroyed. Immediately friends and neighbors took charge and rebuilt their homes.

As Rafe counted the days and months when he could pay the betrothal commitment, he volunteered to help at the Children's Special Needs Center. His fiancée, Mia sulked and complained when she visited him there. She abhorred the unpleasant sight of the sick and disfigured children. Rafe had the opposite sentiment toward those infants and children. He remembered the days when he and Lela were patients at that section of the hospital. They were memorable times.

Without much thought, in the next letter that Lela wrote to Rafe she mentioned her parents' invitation to him, that if he wished to work at another location, a pharmacist was always welcome on Happy Island. After he read Lela's letter Rafe realized that his love for her was worth the risk of venturing into a new life. He sold most of his personal belongings and his extra medical books. Next, he took the money and his savings, a pearl necklace and bracelet, and went to Mia's house. He knelt before Mia's parents and kissed each parent's right hand then rose and presented them the gifts in the most proper ceremonial fashion. While facing them Rafe said," I am sorry but I do not love Mia and I cannot live the rest of my life with someone I do not love." Then he kissed their hands again and walked out the door.

Rafe walked away letting them assume that he left the beautiful, rich Mia for a mere unknown, orphan girl. The next day he submitted his resignation at the hospital and said goodbye to the children and his many friends. He also went and said goodbye to his adopted father, who had disowned him since he began seeing Lela.

Afterward he sailed in a proa heading for Happy Island. He landed at the harbor near Lela's home. When he reached the village where Lela and her family lived, he expected to see a modest home where he would be welcomed. Instead he stood in amazement at the sprawling estate and at the most impressive hacienda facing the ocean.

The family welcomed Rafe in the most hearty manner. He was now to be part of this loving family. With Lela's parents' permission there would soon be a wedding, and that was the way it happened. It was the most elegant and biggest wedding Happy Island ever had, for the most beloved couple. This island would be where children would be raised in the shadows of nurturing parents, grandparents and the ever challenging typhoons.

Glossary

1. Breadfruit – a pulpy fruit of a tree found in the South Seas, baked for food.

2. Pagu – a wild hibiscus tree found in the tropics used for making ropes . . .etc.

3. Proa – a canoe built and used in the Pacific Islands.

4. Typhoon – a cyclone of the W. Pacific Ocean.

Antonia Babauta Lyzenga's first book, Happy Island was published by Xlibris, 2012.

Happy Island and the Typhoons is a sequel. published by Author Reputation Press, 2022.

Lyzenga has three grown children, and is a great grandmother.

She and her husband live in Dayton, NV